Young Learner's

Bernie Gets into Trouble

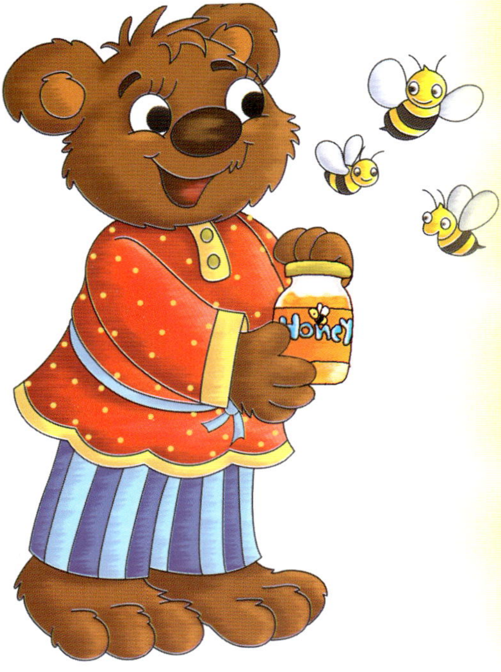

Sangita Koushik

Bernie was a cute little bear. He was naughty and never listened to anyone. And so, his parents were very worried about him.

One day, Bernie's mother bought a bottle of honey. She kept it in the kitchen cupboard. Bernie saw her putting it on the high shelf.

Later, mother said to Bernie, "Son, your father and I are going out to meet some friends. We will be back soon."

She continued, "Please stay away from the honey bottle. You can have the honey once we return."

Bernie nodded his head. Bernie was all alone now. For some time he played in the garden. Soon, he started feeling hungry.

Suddenly, he remembered the honey in the kitchen. He thought, "I am feeling so hungry. I shall eat some honey now. I won't tell mother."

Excitedly, he rushed to the kitchen. As the cupboard was high, Bernie stood on a stool. His little hands touched the bottle of honey.

Bernie was very happy. He slid the bottle closer to himself. But, just as he was about to pick it, the heavy bottle slipped from his little fingers.

"Oh no!" cried out Bernie. To his horror, the bottle came crashing down on the floor.

There were glass pieces all over. The honey spread on the floor. Bernie was in tears.

Now, Mrs. Bee, who was sitting on the window, saw everything. She was very happy. It was feast time!

She quickly brought many of her friends with her. In no time at all, there were bees everywhere!

Bernie tried to be brave. He tried to shoo the buzzing bees away. But they were too many. The bees, in turn, started chasing him.

Bernie was now howling loudly. All this was too much for him! He ran out crying 'Boohoo!' Just then his parents arrived. Bernie told them everything.

They were very angry with Bernie. It took a lot of time for all the bees to be shooed away.

Bernie was ashamed of himself. He promised his parents, "I will never disobey you again."

Moral: Always listen to your elders.